Through Jak's Eyes

by sharon urbia

illustrated by jessalyn toldo

Designed and published by Express Print One, Ltd., Hibbing, Minnesota

Printed in the U.S.A. ISBN 978-1-4276-3125-1

My father's name is Star and my mom's
Apache Moon. My name is Regal Royal Jumpin' Jak
and I was born in Kansas.

My mission – to find someone to love me.

My first home didn't work out, so back to the breeder.

A special couple from Minnesota

wants to adopt me.

I'm going to be princely and cool,
first impressions count – gotta love me!

No more Kansas. Minnesota
"snow" – fun times – mmm – like eating popsicles,
cold on my paws though.

We have a big kennel (RV) for traveling.
Mom is handicapped and this way we
travel and explore.

I'm trying to talk human. I say "I know," "uhuh,"
and "no"; attempting "I love you."

Mom and I howl like wolves and this
helps me vocalize. One of these days
you'll see us on TV.

I'll do tricks for treats, jump through
a hula hoop and polka to "Moja Dekla."
Entertaining is invigorating.

My human sister calls me "Frenchie"
because my breed, Papillion means
"butterfly" in French.

Everyone goes gaga over my butterfly-like,
delicate, frilly, fluttery ears.

"Have fun, will travel," is my motto.
What fun, romping poppy fields and prancing the
yellow bricks at Judy Garland Land.

I've visited an auto museum, a museum
of mining, and "Ironworld USA."

Zoom!

TOURS THIS WAY

While touring, I ride on Mom's lap in her wheelchair "pony". We get a lot of attention.

My life is being a companion dog
to Mom, a home-bound person.

I entertain Mom, walk her and help turn on the computer.
I love hearing, "You've Got Mail."

Mom and I couch. I stay close, protect her,
give kisses and listen to taped books.

I bark for attention and at outside noises.
I sometimes get sent to my naughty corner
–thanks Supernanny!

Talking back doesn't work and
I have "I'm sorry" eyes.

It's my job to alert humans to phone rings, the mail
coming and visitors. This I like,
it makes me feel important and needed.

I'm learning a new language, Slovenian.
New words: "boteeho" (be quiet), "lucka nuch" (good night)
and "lochna" (hungry). I'm bilingual!

They use sign language, spell words
and use "pig Latin," but I'm catching on. I'm smart!

When Mom is fatigued, I lick her feet.

Dad says, "gross!"; Mom says "reflexology."

She's happy, me too.

Another job is Papillion modeling.

Pictures and posing for Dad, and Mom

enters me in contests.

Going to win big–I'm positive.

Therapy work for Dad is something else.
I'm the cross-country running team mascot.

Coach and I watch the team workout
and bring them water. The athletes are dedicated and
I enjoy running around them.

Dad is also the "food and fun" guy.

We car cruise for pleasure.

Coach knows many people and
I perform for their attention.

While ground sniffing, my nose gets glued to one spot.

Dad thinks I have potential to be a hunter.

Therapy dog work is fun,
but difficult!

I wouldn't change my life's work for anything.
I'm one proud therapy dog!